I0691889

George Vasey

George Vasey letters to Walter Deane

1885 - 1893

George Vasey

George Vasey letters to Walter Deane
1885 - 1893

ISBN/EAN: 9783337816308

Printed in Europe, USA, Canada, Australia, Japan

Cover: Foto ©Andreas Hilbeck / pixelio.de

More available books at **www.hansebooks.com**

In sending specimens of plants for investigation it is desirable to have the leaves, flowers, and fruit; and, in the case of bulbous plants, the bulbs, also. When they are sent from a distance it is best to prepare the specimens by drying them under pressure between folds of absorbent paper, otherwise the parts shrink and break so as to be hardly recognizable. When the dried plants are sent they should be protected from breakage in the mail by being inclosed between pieces of stiff pasteboard. Packages weighing less than four pounds can be sent by mail at the rate of one cent per ounce. Write the name of the sender on the outside. In the letter accompanying the specimens state where collected, the date, and any other particulars of the plant, whether reputed poisonous, pestiferous, medicinal, or useful.

UNITED STATES

Department of Agriculture,

BUREAU OF BOTANY,

Washington, D. C., *Feby 10th* 1885.

Mr Walter Deane

Dear Sir'

Your letter of the 8th inst is received. I will reply as well as the books at my command will admit. The genus Limnas is an East Russian one described by Trinius, at least as early as 1824. Probably the grass was discovered by Steller the Russian explorer, as it bears his name (Limnas Stelleri). When Steudel published his Gramineae in 1855, he added Nuttalls genus Greenia to the Limnas of Trin. as a second species, but Mr Bentham in the Genera Plantarum shows that Nuttall's Greenia is not a Limnas, and as the genus Greenia was preoccupied by Wight & Arnolds plant, Mr Bentham establishes the new genus Thurberia for Nuttall's plant. I have not access to the Transactions of the Am. Philosophical Society, in which Nuttall published his name, and therefore cannot decide as to the priority of publication. You will find the works undoubtedly at Cambridge. If Nuttalls plant was published before that of Wight then of course his name should hold, and Wights plant should have another name. Any information I can give you in this line I will cheerfully do —

Truly Yours   Geo. Vasey

In sending specimens of plants for investigation it is desirable to have the leaves, flowers, and fruit; and, in the case of bulbous plants, the bulbs, also. When they are sent from a distance it is best to prepare the specimens by drying them under pressure between folds of absorbent paper, otherwise the parts shrink and break so as to be hardly recognizable. When the dried plants are sent they should be protected from breakage in the mail by being inclosed between pieces of stiff pasteboard. Packages weighing less than four pounds can be sent by mail at the rate of one cent per ounce. Write the name of the sender on the outside. In the letter accompanying the specimens state where collected, the date, and any other particulars of the plant, whether reputed poisonous, pestiferous, medicinal, or useful.

UNITED STATES

Department of Agriculture,

BUREAU OF BOTANY,

Washington, D. C., March 21st 1885.

Mr Walter Dean
Dear Sir

Your letter containing specimen of grasses has been duly received.

With respect to the Festuca I think it is the diuinsula. The other grass at first sight I thought might be Glyceria augustata to which it certainly much resembles, but the structure of the flowers rather places it in Poa. It is a species which I do not recognize, but the specimens are too fragmentary. I hope it will be collected the coming season in complete specimens.

Truly Yours
Geo. Vasey

Department of Agriculture,

Washington, D. C., April 13th, 1885.

Mr Walter Deane
    Dear Sir'

       Yours of the 11 "inst is received.
In reply I have to state that, the supply of the older
Reports of the Department, has long been exhausted,
and they can now be obtained only as occasionally
offered in second hand bookstores, and dealers in antique
books &c. The Reports of the Department, since its separate
organization run back to 1862, previous to that time
there was only an Agricultural Bureau connected with
the Patent Office, and there were Patent Office Reports (Agricultural) running back to 1852.

           Truly Yours
           Geo. Vasey

U. S. Department of Agriculture,

DIVISION OF BOTANY,

Washington, D. C., May 4th 1880.

Mr Walter Deane
　　Dear Sir

　　　　Your letter and the package of grass has been duly received — The grass is Oryzopsis Canadensis Torr. It is a northern grass, being found in New England, New York, Michigan, Wisconsin &c, also I have collected it in the mountains of Colorado —

　　　　　　　　Truly Yours
　　　　　　　　Geo. Vasey

U. S. Department of Agriculture,

DIVISION OF BOTANY,

Washington, D. C., Oct 18th 1886.

Mr Walter Deane

My dear Sir

Yours of the 16th inst containing a specimen for determination has been duly received.

It is difficult to determine with accuracy such specimens without flowers or fruit, but I can give an opinion as to these, and that is that it is Eleocharis Robbinsii in the infertile state. I think if you compare it with specimens of that plant in Herb, Gray, you will find evidence in favor of that view.

Truly Yours

Geo. Vasey

U. S. Department of Agriculture,

DIVISION OF BOTANY,

Washington, D. C., Dec 3 1886.

Mr Walter Deane, Cambridge
   Dear Sir,

         I have examined your package of Texas
Grasses and named them, although 1 or 2 of them are
rather new forms respecting which I have some doubts
which, & will have to be solved in the future, I have added
such of your desiderata as I can now conveniently
find, and hope when I get a little leisure to send you
still others — Thanks for your information about
Dr Gray and Prof. Watson in whom I always feel interested — I hope the good Doctors life may be prolonged
to many years — I enclose with the grasses specimens
of Thurberia Arkansana, and also my "descriptive
Catalogue of grasses" which apparently I had not sent you.

                              Truly yours
                              Geo. Vasey
                              Botanist Dept Agr

U. S. Department of Agriculture,

DIVISION OF BOTANY,

Washington, D. C., March 27' 1888.

Mr Walter Deane
My dear Sir'

Your postal of the 25 "inst. is rec'd.
I have handed in your request for "Information to
wood consumers" to the Forestry Division and it will be
sent you. The "Reports of the U. S. Consuls" are published
by the State Department and you will need to
apply there to obtain them.

Truly Your
Geo. Vasey

P. S. The botanical Section of the Biological Society of this
City have a Memorial Meeting for D Gray next week
April 5th

U. S. Department of Agriculture,

DIVISION OF BOTANY,

Washington, D. C., Nov 14 1888.

Mr Walter Deane
    Cambridge, Mass
        My dear Sir

Your letter of the 12th inst. is at hand. In reply I will state that my address, to which you refer, has not been published. At the Memorial Meeting, 4 addresses were given, and it was proposed to have them all published together, but the funds of the Society seem to have fallen short and Prof. Ward & Dr Riley had theirs otherwise published. Dr. Chickering I think has not had his published—

I can send you mine in Mss if desired.
I can probably also obtain Dr Chickering's for you.

Truly Yours
Geo. Vasey

U. S. Department of Agriculture,

BOTANICAL DIVISION,

Washington, D. C., Feby 14" 1893

Mr Wm Deane
Cambridge Mass
Dear Sir

The Panicum you send is P. viscidum more branched than usual — perhaps an autumnal form. I will try to look up and send you specimens of Sporobolus minor —

Truly Yours
Geo. Vasey

In order to properly estimate the influence which Dr. Gray has exerted upon the progress of botanical science in this country, we must first take a survey of the condition of that science prior to his time. We need not, for this purpose, go farther back than the beginning of the present century. What few botanical works existed prior to that time were very incomplete, and not adapted for study by English readers.

In 1803 the French botanist Michaux, after several years of travel in this country, published in France his Flora of North America. This work applied only to that Atlantic side of the country, and the whole number of species described was about 1500.

In 1814 Mr. F. Pursh published in London a work under the same title as that of Michaux, which contained descriptions of many additional species, principally from the Pacific coast and the Rocky Mountains, increasing the number given to nearly 3000 species. These works were in Latin and published in the old country, more for the benefit of European than of American botanists, but they were almost the only ones then available. It will thus be seen that the opportunities of obtaining a knowledge of botany at this period, for American students were very meagre, and for the common people they did not exist.

But there was really an extraordinary amount of activity and interest in the science springing into life.

Philadelphia and its vicinity was early a centre of botanical research. The botanical gardens of Hamilton, Bartram, Marshall and MacMahon were the repositories of many botanical treasures in the way of trees and shrubs gathered in the journeyings of Michaux, Pursh, Nuttall and others, and a lively interest in botany was diffused among the intelligent and educated part of the population. In 1813 Rev. Dr. Muhlenberg published a catalogue of the plants of North America. In 1818 Mr. Thos. Nuttall, who had been many years engaged in botanical explorations, published at Philadelphia in two small volumes, "The Genera of North American Plants." This, like its predecessors, was in Latin and arranged on the Linnaean system of classification. The faults of this system were well known to Mr. Nuttall, and he was not unacquainted with the efforts which were in progress in Europe to put the science on a scientific basis, but on account of the simplicity and convenience of the system Mr. Nuttall continued its employment.

In the same year, 1818, Dr. Barton, then Professor of Botany in the University of Pennsylvania, published a "Compendium of the Flora of Philadelphia and Environs," which, although imperfect, served as a guide to the botanical students of that region. The first important botanical text-book for this country, in English, was Prof. Eaton's Manual, published at New York in 1818. This was immediately adopted in the principal colleges and academies of the country, and exerted an important influence in the promotion of the science.

Dr. John Torrey became acquainted with Prof. Eaton in New York, and under his guidance rigorously pursued the study of botany, exploring particularly the vicinity of the city of New York.

In 1824 he published the first volume of a "Flora of the Northern and Middle States," and in 1826 a "Compendium of Botany" for the same region. In the Southern States Mr. Elliot, of South Carolina, began the publication of what he modestly called "Sketches of the Botany of South Carolina and Georgia." This was issued in numbers and was not completed until 1824.

In 1822 Mr. Nuttall became Professor of Botany in Harvard University, where, in 1827, he published an "Introduction to the Study of Botany." This was devoted to an account of the structure and physiology of plants and not to the description of species.

But botany had some enthusiastic followers in Boston before Mr. Nuttall was called to his Professorship. In 1814 Dr. Bigelow published an excellent catalogue of the plants in the vicinity of Boston. This work was followed, a few years later, by a work on the medical botany of this country, in three volumes with plates.

In 1836 Dr. Darlington, of Chester County, Pennsylvania published his "Flora Cestrica," which gave exceedingly well written descriptions of the plants of Chester County, and was a great aid to local botanists.

In 1829 Mrs. Lincoln published a small introductory work on botany which rapidly came into use in schools and seminaries. In 1833

Dr. Lewis C. Beck, of Albany, N.Y., published a "Botany of the Northern States," arranged, like all its predecessors, on the artificial system of Linnaeus. In 1830 Dr. John Torrey published an American edition of Dr. Lindley's "Introduction to the Natural System of Botany," which had been issued in London the preceding year. Dr. Torrey had at this time acquired a practical knowledge of plants which placed him at the head of American botanists. He had for many years been sensible of the imperfections of the Linnaean System, and immediately seized the earliest opportunity of presenting to the American student the result of the researches of De Candolle, Jussieu, Lindley, Brown and others.

In the American edition of this work, Dr. Torrey added a catalogue of the North American genera, with the number of species belonging to each genus, as far as they were at that time known, and they amounted to something more than 4000 of phaenogamous plants.

We now approach the point where Dr. Asa Gray makes an appearance in the field of American botany.

In 1833 he made the acquaintance of Dr. Torrey, and this acquaintance was destined to have a controlling interest upon his future life. He took up his residence in the city of New York, and under the efficient guidance of Dr. Torrey he made rapid progress in acquiring a knowledge of the botany of the country. He made botanical excursions in the vicinity of the city, and in various parts of the States of New York and New Jersey, becoming especially interested in the grasses and sedges which were little known, and published some important papers on them, as well as prepared and distributed several sets of specimens in two volumes of one hundred species each.

In 1836 he published the first of the series of his botanical text books. It was entitled "Elements of Botany", and was based upon the writings of De Candolle, Lindley and other European botanists. As an elementary work it was far in advance of the ordinary books of that class, and was creditable to the judgment and scholarship of the author, who was then but twenty-six years old. He now, in connection with Dr. Torrey, began work upon a "Flora of North America," based upon the Natural Method, to be more extensive and complete than anything that had preceded it in this country. This work had long been a subject of thought and purpose by Dr. Torrey, but had been delayed by the press of his business. The first half of the first volume of the new work was published in 1838.

Great difficulty was experienced in settling the proper specific names and synonymy of many plants, especially those of the Pacific coast, from a want of the original specimens upon which the names were founded. It was therefore determined that Dr. Gray should go to Europe to examine the herbariums which contained the types, so that the work might be made accurate. After a year spent in this work, and in making the acquaintance of the most distinguished botanists of the world, Dr. Gray returned to New York and resumed work on the Flora, and the second part of the first volume was completed in 1840. The second volume was chiefly occupied with the natural Order Compositae, the largest and perhaps the most difficult division of flowering plants, and was almost wholly the work of Dr. Gray. It was published in 1842, and the work was then suspended. It became evident that in consequence of the rapid development of the country, particularly in the West, and the acquisition of new territory which was soon to be explored, that the Flora could not be properly completed until a fuller knowledge of the productions of the country could be obtained, and it was determined, therefore, to engage in the elaboration of the plants collected by the various Explorations and Surveys of the Government and of private individuals, and many

years were occupied in these investigations by Drs.
Torrey, Gray, Engelmann, Eaton and others. Early
in the year 1842 Dr. Gray was called to the chair
of botany in Harvard College. He was at that
time engaged in the preperation of a new work
entitled the "Botanical Text-Book," which was published during that year. This volume of over
five hundred pages is divided into two parts,
the first devoted to Structural and Physiological
Botany, and the second to Systematic Botany or the
principles of the classification of plants into genera
and natural orders or families, with brief notices of
their structure, distribution, properties and useful products; each family being illustrated by
figures of some characteristic plant or plants.
This work, as is remarked by Prof. Sargent, was
greatly in advance in scientific value and in lite-
rary finish of any book of similar scope
which had appeared in America and it may
be added also, of any which had appeared
in Europe. It immediately became the leading
book on this subject. It passed through many
editions, each one greatly improved, and the last
one, published in 1879, wholly rewritten.
      In 1847 Dr. Gray sent to press the first
edition of his "Manual of Botany of the Northern
United States." It was designed to give clear
and precise descriptions of all plants which were

Known to grow throughout the northern portion of the country east of the Mississippi River.

This embraced the most populous part of the United States, and was the seat of the best universities, colleges, and higher educational institutions. For the needs of these institutions as well as for the use of private students, Dr. Gray rightly judged that there was existing the need of a work of such a character. Sufficient exploration had been made in this limited region to justify the attempt of the preparation of a Manual, and the success of the effort may be judged from the fact that although the work has passed through six editions in the past forty years, with some modifications and a few additions, yet the general plan of the work has undergone no change, and the number of new species requiring incorporation has been extremely few. Since its first appearance it has been a standard work, adopted in nearly all the colleges and higher institutions, and has exerted great influence upon the progress of botanical science. It was the first descriptive work based on the Natural Method published in this country.

Almost every botanist of note, who has arisen within the past thirty years, has made this book his constant companion and guide, and although it has had competitors, it has, by virtue of its

accuracy, fullness and perspicuity easily taken the
lead, and indeed has been the model after which
others have patterned.

In 1849 Dr. Gray began the publication of
another work, viz: "Illustrations of the Genera
of the North American Flora", in which the
botanical features of each genus were given, and
illustrated and explained by a figure and dis-
sections of at least one species of each genus.
Only two volumes were published, but they were
types of beauty in typographical and artistic
execution. Lack of financial encouragement ne-
cessitated the suspension of the work.

"Gray's Lessons in Botany" was the next ven-
ture toward a complete course of botanical
school books. It was published in 1857
and is an admirable treatise on the principles
of physiological and structural botany. Every
important subject relating to the forms and
manner of growth of plants is here systemati-
cally taken up, and although each item is
brief, it is clean and concise, and there are
illustrations of an excellent character to
explain every important point.

The "Lessons in Botany" were followed the
next year, in 1858, by another elementary
work called "How Plants Grow," and in 1872,
by still another entitled "How Plants Behave".

These are primary works admirably written in a charming style, and adapted to the wants of young beginners in botanical studies, teaching the structure and habits of plants in a familiar manner, guiding the young learner to the observation and love of nature.

In 1868, Dr. Gray published his "Field, Forest and Garden Botany," which is an abridgement of the Manual, with the addition of descriptions of foreign plants common in cultivation in gardens and greenhouses. Teachers of botany especially in cities, were often obliged to resort largely to cultivated plants for illustrations of their lectures, hence there arose a necessity for a work which should include such plants as well as the native ones. It was also a work required by florists and horticulturists. This work was also bound with the "Lessons in Botany", under the title of "School and Field Botany".

We have thus mentioned the botanical works embraced in the series for the use of schools and colleges. They are the result of great labor, but they represent only a small part of the untiring and protracted investigations of the plants their distinguished author

The labor connected with the identification

of the plants collected, in the Explorations and Surveys of the Government and of private individuals was protracted through many years, and engaged not only the attention of Dr. Torrey until his death in 1873, but the constant, unremitting study of Dr. Gray.

These investigations are represented by various publications of which we can scarcely give more than the titles of the principal ones.

"Plantae Fendlerianae" is an account of the collections of Mr. August Fendler in New Mexico in 1846. It describes seventeen new genera and many new species.

"Plantae Wrightianae" is a description of the plants collected in New Mexico and Texas by Mr. Chas. Wright, published in 1849. It describes sixteen new genera.

"Plantae Thurberianae" is an account of the plants collected by Mr. George Thurber in Western Texas, New Mexico and Arizona.

"Plantae Lindheimerianae" gives an account of the plants collected in Western Texas by Mr. F. Lindheimer. Beside these, there are various extensive reports on the plants collected during the Mexican Boundary Survey, on the several Pacific Railroad Surveys, and other government explorations. which are all well known, and need not be separately mentioned.

But Dr. Gray's researches were
to North American plants. In 183
ment, after several years of delay,
naval expedition under the comma
afterwards Admiral. Wilkes, ostensibly
pose of making deep sea soundings
Hemisphere. Dr. Gray had been
botanist of this expedition, but the
delays prevented his acceptance of the
expedition occupied five years in
tions and made extensive natural hi
tions at all the points of landing.
who accompanied the expedition we
Rich, of Georgetown, D.C., Mr. Bracke
of Baltimore, and Dr. Pickering, of
The large botanical collections of
men were placed in the hands of
elaboration. With his usual indus
resolution he worked in this new
prepared a report, of which only
a fine quarto of 777 pages, accor
a folio atlas of 100 plates was pu
1854. This volume embraced our
petalous plants, and contained desc
sixteen new genera and about two
and fifty new species.
Beside the above mentioned wo

lished by Dr. Gray in various American and foreign journals.

Few persons can fully comprehend the immense amount of labor involved in these protracted works. Many thousand specimens had to be carefully examined, a large portion of which were entirely new to science, new genera had to be constructed and their proper position in the Natural System ascertained

When at length the surveys and explorations were chiefly brought to a close, and the great influx of novelties had somewhat subsided, Dr. Gray again entered upon the work which for thirty years had been the dream of his ambition namely, the Flora of North America —

But the two volumes already published, had now to be rewritten to incorporate the new genera and species, in many cases to eliminate and correct errors which the advance of science had exposed, and so to classify and arrange the material as to avoid all unnecessary descriptive matter, and yet to record every characteristic point needful to the recognition of a species. Yet, in Dr. Gray's judgment, it was more needful for the wants of botanical students that he should begin first where he had left off, and prepare an account of the gamopetalous plants.

This volume was completed and published in 1878 under the title of "The Synoptical Flora of North America".

He then retraced his steps to rewrite the second volume, which comprised the immense Order of Compositae. To do this required another visit to Europe to consult the European herbariums in order to unravel the confusion of synonymy and to authenticate the species which had been established by the earlier botanists. After six years of labor the work on this volume was completed in 1884.

In the interval of time between these volumes, the researches of foreign botanists regarding the priority of certain generic names had made some changes necessary. Some large and difficult genera were divided, and new generic names established or older ones restored. These changes were noticed by Dr. Gray from time to time in the scientific journals, but they accumulated to such a proportion that he deemed it necessary to publish a supplement to the two volumes, embodying many additions, and adapting the changes and modifications to their proper places, in order to bring the work fully up to the advanced standing of the science. This Supplement comprises nearly fifty pages.

The great work upon which his heart was set was now half completed, and with unabated zeal, but with diminishing physical energy he addressed himself to the continuation of his task. Several years have been given to rewriting the volume on Polypetalae, and botanists were eagerly awaiting its appearance, but its author did not live to see its completion. But the material is in a forward state, and, in the hands of his colleagues, it is believed, will be shortly ready for publication.

Not alone in analytic and descriptive powers did Dr. Gray excel. He possessed remarkable ability for synthesis and comprehensive reasoning, as is shown in many of his reviews and public addresses. His admirable and scholarly paper on the "Parallels of the Flora of Japan and North America", tracing the common origin of the two floras down to the tertiary epoch, placed him in the front rank as a scientific thinker.

His address delivered before the British Association for the Advancement of Science, in session at Montreal, in August, 1884, upon the "Characteristics of the Flora of North America", was an able paper, and added to his fame as a comprehensive and original reasoner

His celebrated discussion of the doctrine of evolution, and his papers on the Darwinian theory, will be brought to your attention by other speakers.

Dr. Gray felt great interest in the National Herbarium in the Department of Agriculture, in this city. Being one of the Regents of the Smithsonian Institution, he generally attended their annual meetings, and at such times, as well as at other opportunities, he was accustomed to the visit the Herbarium and to spend as much time as he could in examining the collection, and in giving assistance to the botanist in charge. A large part of the plants were types which had formerly passed under his hands, and their security and preservation were to him objects of solicitude.

There remains to me but to make some concluding observations, to make apparent the great development of botany during the past fifty years.

The Catalogue of North American plants given by Dr. Torrey in his edition of Lindley's Introduction to Botany in 1831, enumerates 4081 species of phaenogamous plants as the number then known. This number was not greatly increased when, two years later, Dr. Gray joined Dr Torrey in his botanical labors. The most recent enumeration of the plants of the same region is about 11000 species, embraced in 1665 genera. Of these, eighty-five genera have been named by Dr. Gray, and, of the total number of species, about 2000 have received names from his hand.

The most striking point in the consideration of Dr. Gray's labors is the complete revolution which has been effected in the System of Classification. The earlier works were all constructed on the Linnaean System, and for many years after Doctors Torrey and Gray began their introduction of the Natural Method, some school books continued to be published on the old plan, but all such have been long since abandoned. As an indication of the popularity of Dr. Gray's school books, I have the statement from his publishers that there have been sold, in round numbers, 500 000 volumes.

The history of Dr. Gray for the past fifty years is practically the history of North American Botany for that period.

Many other honorable names are associated with his as contributors and helpers

in special lines of study. No man knew
better than he the breadth and extent of
the great field in which he was laboring,
and the need of many observers and students.
By all his co-workers and associates, as
well as his numberless correspondents, the
memory of Dr. Gray will be honored and
revered on account of his urbanity and
kindness of heart, his willingness to impart
information and afford assistance to in-
vestigators, and to encourage by his example
the most critical and thorough research.

— " —

An address delivered at the Gray Memorial Meeting
of the Botanical section of the Biological Society
of Washington D.C., April 5th, 1888.